THE Storybook Knight

Story by
Helen Docherty

sourcebooks
jabberwocky

Illustrated by
Thomas Docherty

Leo was a gentle knight
in thought and word and deed.
While other knights liked fighting,
Leo liked to sit and read.

He was kind to every creature.
He wouldn't hurt a fly.

When Mom and Dad said,
"Knights must FIGHT!"

he couldn't quite see why.

One morning, Leo's parents said
they'd like to have a chat.
There was nothing wrong with reading,
but he couldn't *just* do that!

They'd seen an ad that morning
in their favorite magazine.
A dragon needed taming!
Leo wasn't very keen.

"Nonsense! You'll enjoy it.
It'll stop you getting bored.
In case the dragon's scary,
here's a brand-new shield and sword."

Leo packed some sandwiches.
(And lots of books, of course.)

Then with a sigh, he saddled up
Old Ned, his faithful horse.

He hadn't traveled far
(though the sun had risen high),
when suddenly, a fearsome creature
swooped down from the sky.

It had a lion's body,
but it had an eagle's wings.

"A griffin!" marveled Leo,
who had read about such things.

"Come on," snarled the griffin,
"I dare you to a fight!"

"I'd rather not," said Leo.
"It wouldn't be quite right.

I've got my brand-new
sword with me,
so I'd be bound to win it.

"But how about a story
with some pictures
of *you* in it?"

"Yes, please!" the griffin nodded.
(He was really rather vain.)

So Leo read a book to him—
once, twice,
and then again.

"It's yours to keep," said Leo
as he clambered back on Ned.
"Oh, thank you!" cried the griffin,
and he bowed his noble head.

Leo rode for hours,
though the heat was quite extreme…

then stopped to have his picnic
by a welcome mountain stream.

"Who dares to trespass on my bridge?"
inquired a hungry troll.

"It's only me," said Leo.
"Would you like to share my roll?"

The troll just laughed.
"No thanks," he growled.
"I think I'll just eat YOU!"

But Leo said, "My armor's
pretty difficult to chew.

"I've got a brilliant book though,
if you'll hang on just a minute…
It's full of juicy goats and, look!
It's even got *you* in it."

"Hmm, that sounds good,"
   the troll replied,
his hunger put on hold.
So Leo read the story
(with some changes,
   truth be told).

"It's yours to keep," said Leo
as he clambered back on Ned.
"Oh, thank you!"
    cried the grateful troll,
and bowed his heavy head.

Leo kept on riding
through that long, hot afternoon.
At last, he came upon a town
as empty as the moon.

The leaves were burnt on every tree,
the grass and flowers too.

He'd seen some messy streets before,
but *this* was something new.

Faces peered from windows:
folks too scared to go outside.
He trotted bravely onward.
"Hey, watch out!" the people cried.

What he saw around the corner
set him shaking in his shoes:
the most ENORMOUS dragon,
who'd just woken from a snooze.

The dragon raised his eyebrows.
"Not another pesky knight!"
"Don't worry!" Leo told him,
"I haven't come to fight.

"I've got the most amazing book
with loads of dragons in it.

But it's going in the trash
unless you clean up right this minute!"

"Oh, don't do that!" the dragon cried,
"I'll clean it up right now!
But I'm really bad at tidying.
Perhaps you'll show me how?"

So Leo taught the dragon
how to shovel,
scoop, and clear.

And, one by one, the townsfolk
all began to lose their fear.

"*Now* can I have my story?"
begged the dragon
on his knees.

So Leo read the book six times.
(A dragon's hard to please.)

"It's yours to keep," said Leo
as he clambered back on Ned.
"Oh, thank you," cried the dragon,
and he bowed his scaly head.

When Leo reached his home at last,
the cheers were long and loud.
His parents hugged him very tight.
"Well done! You've made us proud."

Now Leo is a hero,
His parents have agreed…

He doesn't have to fight at all.
He's left in peace—to read.

For Helen's dad, Gareth (another gentle knight), and for our very own Leo.
Also for Wilf, Felix, Laurie, Jake, Max, and Edward.

First published in the United States in 2016 by Sourcebooks
Text © 2016, 2021 by Helen Docherty
Illustrations © 2016, 2021 by Thomas Docherty
Cover and internal design © 2016, 2021 by Sourcebooks

Sourcebooks and the colophon are registered trademarks of Sourcebooks.

The full color art was created with acrylic ink and hot-pressed watercolor paper.

Published by Sourcebooks Jabberwocky, an imprint of Sourcebooks Kids
P.O. Box 4410, Naperville, Illinois 60567-4410
(630) 961-3900
sourcebookskids.com

Originally published as *The Knight Who Wouldn't Fight* in 2016 in the United Kingdom by Alison Green Books, an imprint of Scholastic Children's Books.

Library of Congress Cataloging-in-Publication Data is on file with the publisher.

Source of Production: Wing King Tong Paper Products Co. Ltd., Shenzhen, Guangdong Province, China
Date of Production: October 2022
Run Number: 5028765

Printed and bound in China.
WKT 10 9 8 7